The Un-Inquired

The Un-Inquired

Renee Chen

Querencia Press, LLC
Chicago Illinois

QUERENCIA PRESS

© Copyright 2024
Renee Chen

All Rights Reserved

No reproduction, copy or transmission of this publication may be made without
written permission.
No paragraph of this publication may be reproduced, copied or transmitted
save with the written permission of the author.

Any person who commits any unauthorized act in relation to this publication
may be liable to criminal prosecution and civil claims for damages.

ISBN 978 1 959118 55 8

www.querenciapress.com

First Published in 2024

Querencia Press, LLC
Chicago IL

Printed & Bound in the United States of America

This book is dedicated to all the people I have encountered in my life, and to those struggling to find their voice in society.

CONTENTS

The Unspoken Words 11

The Finitey of Time 24

Place of Milk 32

The Neverlands 38

Kaguya 54

The Unspoken Words

I.

Kuroda, not my father, was the one who taught me how to play baseball.

He was the one whom I watched, emulated, and worshiped as a child before the television—black cap on the head and the overlapped letters of NY in sleet-white.

"He's Hiroki, and I'm Hiro," I told my sister once, hands splayed out in the air as if receiving applause. "We're connected. Can't you see?"

"Just first names, moron," she said and stole the remote control from my hand, switching over to the movies channel. I ran upstairs into my room and grabbed a bundle of pillows, tossing them into the air to send them across the hallway with my plastic bat, aiming for her face.

"Three strikes out," she yelled after catching my balls. I stuck my tongue out at her. It wasn't how baseball worked in real-life, but those were always the rules to her.

Three strikes out.

II.

My sister Amber and I are twins. My parents like to tell others that we were born as mono-mono twins, that we had shared the same amniotic sac and placenta in a liminal space that was both life and not life.

Before the two of us were out of my mother's womb, my parents had planned to give us Japanese names. For a while, in market chit-chats and office coffee breaks, my name was Hiro. Hiro for tolerance and Hiro for generosity, and my sister was Yōko, for the sun and all the light that ensues.

Within weeks of my birth, my parents learned that I had albinism and they decided to change my name into Hiroyuki, or white Hiro. In the end, they didn't. Instead, like so many families in and out of Kingman, we got American names that didn't fit with our Japanese last name. We became Aiden and Amber Enomoto. Like complementary colors, our first and last names were each other's strongest contrast.

III.

Around the time when I was starting kindergarten, my mother told me the story of Yuki-onna. It was one of those days when she was in an obvious good mood and would have my sister and me sit on either side of her on the tatami while she spelled out tales of Momotarō and Kaguya, boys born from peaches and princesses from the moon—tales that were both whimsical and real.

Splayed out on bed that afternoon, she told us that Yuki-onna was a ghost, dazzling with a pair of zircon-blue eyes and pitch-black hair.

"She wears a white kimono," my mother told us, dragging her voice to make herself sound eerie, "and hunts for travelers on the mountains to kill."

"Why is she called Yuki-onna?" My sister asked, her head slumped in between her two hands, her elbows on her knees.

"Because Yuki means white in Japanese," she told us. I stared at my fingers, powder-white skin, lighter than the tip of my nails. "And onna means woman." She stood up from the floor, stretching her hands.

"If I were a girl, would I be Yuki-onna?" I asked my mother, but she had already walked away.

IV.

I got my first baseball bat, a wooden—not plastic—one, on my ninth birthday. Amber was the one who bought it for me. After our parents had gotten us two sets of Monopolies as our boons, she traded them with the boy living across from our house.

When I thanked her, the weight of the gift pressed against my chest, a light sense of coolness emanating out of its wooden skin, she petted me on my shoulder.

"I don't like Monopoly anyways," she shrugged and walked away.

That first afternoon after I received the gift, I found an abandoned construction site near my house. It was the practice field of a group of neighborhood children, where baserunners slid across knee-deep ash, under the cheers, the arrogance of childhood dreamers.

"You can play?" one of them, a boy wearing a white, striped Yankees cap, shouted from across the field.

I nodded. He tossed a ball over, and I swung my bat in the air. My eyes traced the ball's perfect trajectory across the field. He smiled when he walked over, reaching his hand out.

"Sam," he said, giving me a brief nod.

I took off my cap and fanned it against my face, the summer heat draining down from the sky. "Aiden," I told him.

V.

I stopped sharing the same room with Amber at the age of five, the summer when her first outbursts started.

Every day for three months, I would wake at midnight to hear her screaming on the bed next to mine and try to shield myself from her shrieks as my parents ran into our room to take her out. Within months, midnight screams became no more to my ears than drips of water against melamine plates in our kitchen sink.

"Why do you scream?" I finally asked her one morning, when we were sitting on the veranda outside the living room. We were eating shaved ice, the cloying syrup rose-pink against the grains of ice.

"Because there are ghosts in this house," she said.

I licked my lips. "What do they look like?"

"White, like shadows," she said, closing her eyes to picture them. "No legs, or hands. More like clusters of mist."

I crunched the ice in my mouth.

"Let's catch them," she told me, suddenly turning around and looking me in the eyes. "Let's do it tonight, Hiro."

"Aight," I said.

VI.

The first time my parents took Amber to a pediatrician, they were brushed aside. "You have to stop spoiling that girl," my grandmother yelled at them across the telephone. "What do you mean she won't eat anything but pancakes? This is ridiculous."

In her room, Amber sat still next to me, breathing in and out quickly. That night, after our promise, I had stayed up late and sneaked into her room at a quarter past one. I had almost dozed off, lying on the rug beside her bed, but she woke me up just when I was falling asleep.

"There," she told me, pointing ahead. I stared at the curtains in front of us, lace polka dots in blue and green. "You see it?"

I blinked hard. I closed my eyes, opened them, then started all over again.

She pinched my cheek, "You still awake?" My lips parted, but no words came out. "It's there—" she said, standing up on her bed, clutching onto a pillow, "the ghost."

I didn't see anything.

The lights above us blinked on, the night silent. I stared at the curtains as Amber started to scream and pull her own hair.

"It's coming for me—" she yelled, cried. "The ghost—the ghost—"

I covered my ears with my hands instinctively as she slumped down into her bed, kicked her blanket onto my face, shrieked and cried. My parents ran in. When my mother saw me in the room, my eyes still on the curtains, she slapped me in the face.

VII.

Before Amber left the house, the two of us shared a puzzle box that we had found one evening in the attic. It is a birchwood box our grandfather had designed, his name imprinted on the lacquer that ran across its patterns of hazel spirals and red squares. For a while, Amber and I kept it under her bed, buried in the dust.

Inside the puzzle box, we stored bamboo-copters and paper cranes. At night, lying on our stomachs on the floor, we blew up paper balloons, played with the kendama, the red ball dancing up and down in the air.

One time, I decided to show her some magic. I grabbed two paper cups from the kitchen and a red strand of yarn from my mother's knitting kit. I taped the string onto the bottom of the two cups and told her to hold onto one, put it next to her ear. Then, standing two meters away from her, I whispered into the cup.

"Can you hear me? Amber—"

Two meters away, her eyes widened. She grinned and tucked the cup against her face. "Can you hear me?" She asked. "Hiro—Hiro—Hiro?"

I held the cup next to my ear firmly and tried to track the movement of our words down the strand of yarn but couldn't see anything. I let her call my Japanese name over and over again as I stared at the string, the only thing that was tying the two of us together across the room. The grasp of the string improbably frail, like so many things.

VIII.

Sam and I were the two youngest players in our school's baseball team, the underdogs, as he liked to say. We practiced almost daily after school, tossing the ball back and forth in his yard, battering at the construction site. In our own games, I was always the pitcher, and he the batter.

For a while, flinging the ball across the field, my eyes fixed on Sam, I would feel sweat wash my skin away, its sleet-whiteness tanned in dirt. The cap would press my silver hair down, until each strand was drowned in linns of sunshine.

The first time he came over was for a sleepover. I took him to my room at the end of the hallway on the second floor of our house. We had raced up the stairs, pretending that we were baserunners, and slid across the marble floor. We sprang into my room, and as we leapt onto the bed, Amber walked in.

"This place is awesome," Sam told me, his legs crossed on my bedsheets. There were posters of Babe Ruth, Lou Gehrig, and Yogi Berra on the wall before us, crayon-drawn sketches of the baseball field and Yankees logo. There was a basket, once used for laundry, beside my bed. Within it were ten baseball bats, three plastic and the rest wooden.

Amber walked into the room, her footsteps light and muffled against the carpet. "Get off my bed," she said.

"Your bed?" Sam eyed me. I shrugged.

"He's Sam, Amber," I told her, hopping down from the bed. "My friend from school." I gave Sam a shove with my elbow. "She's Amber, my sister."

"I'm not Amber," she said. "I'm Parasite Mind."

"That's her nickname," I told him before Sam could ask more. But Amber stormed across the room to us and corrected me. "It's not my nickname. It's my name."

I felt my ears burning red. "Alright, just leave us for now, Amber."

"I'm not Amber," she told me again. Sam shifted next to me, his back straightened. "And you're not supposed to be on this bed. Scott likes to sleep here."

"Who's Scott?" Sam asked.

"My cat," Amber told him, her eyes fixed on mine.

He turned to me, "You have a cat?" I shook my head. We didn't have a cat. Scott was Amber's imaginary pet. Before Scott, she had a bunny named Three-hundred. When Three-hundred died, Amber locked herself in her room and wouldn't come out for two days. My parents had to call a locksmith to get her out. The problem was, Three-hundred was Amber's imaginary pet too.

"Do me a favor," I told Sam after the two of us had left the room to Amber. We were sitting on the carpet in the living room, tossing a baseball ball back and forth in the air. "Don't tell anyone," I said, taking my baseball mitt off, "that I have a sister."

IX.

At first, I didn't know what schizophrenia was.

For weeks, I visited the local library and tried to understand it by reading anything I could find—science magazines, peer-review journals, medical textbooks—burning through the words and sentences on each page to find an answer. Yet, I was disappointed.

Even now, we still don't know. The causes of schizophrenia remain a mystery. Less than one percent of the population has ever developed the disorder.

"So you're saying that my daughter is crazy?" my mother asked the doctor.

He spun his pen between his fingers and looked at my parents for a long time. "Not crazy, ma'am," he said, but nothing else.

Sitting on the swiveling chair next to my parents, I poked at my jeans. Amber had tried to choke herself the night before her appointment with the doctor.

"Why?" I had screamed at her. She was strangling herself with her jacket, the sleeves tied around her neck.

"Because I don't want to live," she said.

X.

When I started middle school, I stopped calling Amber on the telephone. When my parents visited the psychiatric hospital she was staying in, I stayed behind at home, watching baseball on television. When they asked, I told my classmates that I was an only child who desperately wanted a brother to play baseball with.

In my junior year in high school, I got a fracture in the fibula and had to stay in the hospital for two days. Amber came to visit me, at the doctor's permit. Only then, when she stepped into the tiny hospital room, staring at the checkerboard tiles on the floor like she was playing chess on it, did I realize how much she'd changed. Her hair had darkened and grown longer, now in straight strands down her slim back. When I saw her, I picked at my own hair, the whiteness that was impossible to dye.

"Hey," I told Amber when she looked down at me. I glimpsed at her from the corner of my eye then glanced away.

It seemed as if time had thieved bits of my memories away, and all of a sudden, I couldn't conceive of what we used to talk about as kids. I laid still on the bed, sweating beneath white sheets that smelled like antiseptics. She didn't say anything.

"Hey, are you mad at me or something?" I asked her. Her eyes were fixed on the ceiling, and I studied it for a moment.

Amber didn't say anything, she just kept her head faced up at the fading white paint above us.

"Amber?" I asked. When she turned around to look at me, she stared straight into my eyes. For a moment, when her mouth opened, I thought she was going to scream at me for leaving her. But she didn't.

She closed her mouth again. And neither of us spoke for the rest of the hour.

XI.

At medical school, I studied biochemistry, embryology, and anatomy; I took all the available classes, everything and nothing but neuro and behavioral science.

For a while, I enjoyed college's craziness. I went to naked parties and took up drinking, topping beer that tasted more or less like caramel. Aprils came and classmates asked me about cherry blossoms and Japan, whether the sakuras there were like these in Connecticut. Eventually, I got tired of explaining that I had never really been to Japan and was raised in Kingman, and no, Kingman is not really in the middle of a desert. It also snows there.

XII.

The winter I got my license as a surgical oncologist, my mother called me and told me that Amber had died. She had jumped off a bridge after she broke out of the mental hospital at midnight.

The next day, I took a five-day break from my work. When my colleagues asked where I was going, I said that one of my friends had died in a car accident at home.

The funeral was set up in a tiny, bone-white church. Most of those who went were family members I'd never seen before. As the crowd spread their condolences to my parents, I stayed at the last bench at the back of the church away from everyone, eyes closed to shut myself off from the rest of the world.

Before I knew it, I was hyperventilating in the cold air. White clouds of breath came out of my mouth, at first in strings, then all at once. Slowly, they clotted into a humanoid, the snow and the void between snow, and erupted into life. And then there it was, right in front of me: the world's loneliest ghost.

XIII.

After the funeral, I found a telephone booth near the church and went in, counting the coins left in my jeans pocket. I tucked my fingers against its cool, rusted buttons and held the phone against my ears, still thinking about the song that they were playing back at the church. It sounded familiar. Was it *You Raise Me Up*?

As static emanated out of the phone and strings of noises dimmed in and out, I waited, drumming my fingers against the glass wall. When the dots of buzzes faded out, I pushed another coin in, then another, and another. Rain had started pouring down against the walls of the booth, but I kept on waiting. Perhaps, a part of me is still waiting now.

The Finitey of Time

You were the one who told me about the ancient tale from China of two lovers who died for each other. That night, we were sitting on the cold roof of our school building, looking out into the darkness rippling across the bare campus. Blinking neon lights lit up the streets. Was it only me, or did the night also remind you of potpourri? How all the screaming lights and colors in the city were nothing more than taxidermies, decapitated on electronic screens.

"Do you know what happened after they died?" you asked me. My head was still against yours, my face warm, almost hot, the circuit of blood within me crackling with flames.

The door of the sports equipment storage room smelled of rust, of iron and blood. I shook my head against you.

"Do you know how light *flits* sometimes?"

"Flits?" I thought about butterflies with my eyes closed, wings-breath away from breaking for every flap against the blurred sky.

You continued, "Light flitted out of their graves, and two peacocks flew out."

I closed my eyes, trying to imagine. "They must have been beautiful."

"I bet so." You swayed your head, moving lightly from left to right. "They were in love, after all," you said.

I smiled. You were already beautiful before you fell in love.

***

When I met you, I must have been twelve. You were wearing a yellow dress, the color of sparkling lemonade fizzes caught at the tongue. In the art gallery, under warm-hued lighting, your leather shoes thudded against the wooden hall, like the rat-a-tat of pulse against one's chest. You stopped by a white-framed photo of the Palace of Versailles.

The two of us were the only students at the exhibit and when you saw me you walked over, your dress flitting in the air-conditioned room.

"Hi," you said, smiling as you reached your hand out. "I'm Chinatsu."

Under the dim lights, your brown hair, tied in a short ponytail, was three shades brighter than the rest of your face, porcelain skin and glass eyes, dark and deep.

I took your hand, "Kaito Hoshino."

"Hoshino?" You smiled, your eyes on the wooden ceiling. Your bangs shadowed the gray birthmark beneath your left eyebrow. "That's a beautiful name."

I shrugged.

"It means a field of stars, doesn't it?"

"Think so," I said. "And yours—Chinatsu. That's a thousand summers, right?"

"Rebirth and permanence, yes," you told me. A name beyond human flesh.

***

On my birthday, the first one we celebrated together, you gave me a feather pen. It was peacock, green watercolor shades with a zircon eyespot at the center.

"You know? Feathers take up sixty-percent of a peacock's body weight," you said, holding the pen up to the flickering overhead light dusting shelves of books. Cross-legged on the soft library rug, I looked up at it with you. It made me think about sunlight in forests, rays glinting between foliage and twigs.

"A cost for beauty," I said and took the pen from you, smoothing the cool zircon with my fingers. "These eyespots—I've heard they're actual crystals."

You nodded, "Probably why their feathers are so heavy."

"Probably why they almost never fly," I said.

***

Back then, I told you a lot of lies. Some I now regret. Some I still don't know how to confess. You once told me that people lie not out of malice, but to mask their insecurities, that it's a way of drawing a sword back rather than thrusting it out.

Perhaps I was only drawing back my sword when I told you why I wanted to be a writer. Because I was thirteen, and the Earth was four billion years older.

Do you remember that one morning, a few weeks after our first encounter at the art exhibit, when we met again at the old bookstore your father worked in? It wasn't the first time I had found myself lingering by the dust-coated windows of the shop, lost among shelves of damp books. But it was the first time I saw you there, clad in a sapphire blue apron, dusting off the novels of Natsume Kinnosuke.

When you saw me, you smiled. "You're Hoshino, right?"

"Yes, we met at the art gallery last time," I said, smiling. Your hair was caramel-brown under the ripples of the awakening summer sun. You climbed onto a rusted ladder and started cleaning the books in the upper shelves. I picked up a blank leather notebook from atop the stationaries on display. Its cover, like shadowed water in ocean trenches.

"You write?" you asked me, facing the mahogany shelves as you talked.

I nodded, returning the book.

"A writer then?"

I crossed my arms, "A writer? I guess so. I write the unspoken words, the ones you can't say. Or at least that's what I tell others."

"The unspoken words?" you asked, stepping down from the ladder.

"Things not said soon enough," I told you, "things we forget to say."

"So, you write to erase your regrets?"

"Oh hmm," I said, "I never thought about it this way, but I guess so. But not my regrets— it's this world's regrets."

You smiled. "That must be a lot of books."

***

Sometimes, when I write with the feather pen, splayed out on the grass of the empty university campus, beneath shadows of exhaust and the jags of skyscrapers, I think about you.

I close my eyes and picture myself under a night where there are stars instead, glimmers like the peacock's eyespot in between my hands. I think about the things I'd tell you if you were still here, about the zircon—the closest thing I know to the dazzle of your eyes.

***

Back at school, the only things I knew more about than you did were books and authors.

"What do you think Natsume Kinnosuke wrote for?" I once asked you, staring at the constellations of Leo and Andromeda. For a moment or so, sitting in the air-conditioned planetarium, holding your hand in mine, it seemed to make no difference that I was not lying under actual stars that would one day collapse on their own gravity and bloat only to die again, but permanent footages that were dead already from the moment they were taken from the sky.

You sank down in your seat. "I don't know. But I'd guess a lot of writers write to be remembered." You made a triangle with your hands and thrust it out into the air, trying to match it with Altair, Deneb, and Vega on the screen. "To be permanent, I guess. Embalmed and passed down."

***

When you had your first heart attack, you were five years old.

At the hospital a few avenues away from our school, after your second attack you confided, "Sixty-nine percent of infants born with CDHs can live to eighteen years old." The room was freezing, the engines of the air conditioner churning above us. I sat still on the tiled floor, holding your hand in mine.

"You'll make it past that," I told you and thought about E.E. Cummings, about what it would be like to carry a heart within your own.

You shrugged. "I'll still have four more years."

"You'll have more than that," I said, softly.

"Maybe four years would suffice."

Your hand felt light in mine, light like a feather. So, I held onto it tightly, fighting the fear that it would slip away.

***

For years, I couldn't forget you.

Like a hatchling that still needed the warmth of its mother, I was not ready to lose you yet. I dreamt about you most nights, the two of us standing under the winter sky, where every muffled breath, every tongued word, was turning gossamer white in the air, freezing and dying in haze. And while I stood there in the falling snow that was growing into a storm, you lay still on the ground, resting on the ice-coated land into a long sleep.

***

Before your family flew over to Honshu, you lived in Ishigaki, an island far off from where the rest of Japan is. It had a boundless sea of emerald you told me once—transparent, the surface of the water thin like air.

But what you liked the best about the place was always the sea above you. The sky of stars and the Milky Way and the light and the darkness, the blue that altered a little every night, the distant clouds of celadon green, glazes that made nights a little less dark, made evenings flash by.

Sometimes, when the silence of the dark pecks into my ears, I wonder what it would be like if I too grew up on the island instead of Osaka. What was it like? Running across the summer sand and

30

feeling the bites of the sun in between your toes, listening to the click of your straw sandals against the asphalt bridge, white as slate across a skyline that had no lines? What was it like, Chinatsu, to live in a world without me?

***

When I went to a university in Tokyo alone, I brought with me the feather pen you once gave me. Last night as I was looking out of my window into the blazing traffic lights beneath me, I started thinking about you again.

Holding the quill in between my fingers, its tip resting on the last page of my blue leather notebook, ink in drizzles across the page, I thought about what you said a long time ago at the planetarium.

Perhaps, we don't write to be remembered, but write to remember instead.

Lying in bed last night, I remembered what you'd said for a long, long time.

Place of Milk

There was a time when there wasn't war, when red meant roses, and not the wounds of a body, the tingling surge of some things missing, tides of blood out of a broken skin. It was a time when ears still knew music, singing voices and the ebullient magic of them, not the shots made by guns.

I wasn't born into the war, but my brother was. Around the same age I learned about the fearful avidity before stepping into a river, pants rolled up and tanned skin fondling the water, he learned about a country that was torn apart and sewn back together, stared with his newborn eyes at the seam left behind, jagged scar on the face of an entire people.

In summer afternoons when heat drained down from the sky, like the weight of clothes pressed against the line, the two of us would leave our tents to the adjacent fields. We would race against each other, past timber planks that bridged creeks thick with runoff, plastic blue tents coated in mold, cans and glass bottles that, like dandruff, dotted dirt paths. Perhaps all the time, scuttling and gasping into the wind, we had really been racing against the world.

"We lived in a house," I would tell him when we rested our heads against our knees, t-shirts clinging to our chests. "Not a tent." I drew it out on the soil, the heat flickering against my finger. "We lived in a town called Nyamata. Not Zaire."

"Nyamata," he would repeat the name to himself quietly, feeling the weight of the word against his tongue. "Place of milk."

"The place of milk," I said, the heels of his feet pressed against mine. It was what the word meant in Kinyarwanda, our language. "It's why Dad named you Amata," I told him.

And also why I always called him Milk.

***

Before my mother died giving birth to Amata, we lived in a tall, narrow house with celadon green roofs. It was the most novel, eccentric one in the town, my father had told me—one with orange-plastered walls and grand casement windows in sapphire blue, birchwood frames.

Inside the house, enveloped between the tang of salted broth and stewed plantains, was a kitchen, where I had once listened, humming, to the drums of a metal spoon against a pot, the whacks of a blade against an onion, sliced away like trees chopped by swinging axes.

"There is a whale who brought me out of the sea," my mother would sing, her caramel hair tied in a ponytail, the curls cuddled to her back, "and took me to a land where a man met me. We went to a castle, and all was meant to be. There was a door to happiness, and you were the key."

***

The first night when the gunshots came, zigzagged across the flatness of tin-roofed houses, pricks of Acacia flower buds, crumbled and collapsed onto dirt-doorsteps, my father was away at the hospital. He was there finishing his night shift as doctor when he hurtled home and took my brother and me to our bedroom at the center of the house.

For hours, I sat shadowed by his silhouette, stared at the flecks of moonlight on his thick, boxy glasses. I could feel the crisping chill from the birchwood planks that made up the floor beneath me, the lacquer thin and glassy, like grass glazed by dew. He hummed to Amata softly, my brother in his arms and the lights above us turned off. Somewhere, someone hollered against destiny.

At midnight, he woke me up. There was a sack on his shoulder, scattered clothes on the bed, splayed out like mustard seeds frying in a pot. But I couldn't see any steam. "We need to leave," he told me.

I looked to where mother was buried, "But what about Mom?"

He opened the door of the room, his bronze fingers curled around the doorknob. "She'll be here," he told me, taking my hand in his. We strode out of the house, the darkness descending above us. The patches of clouds were thick, the heat choking the air, its weight like a wet towel. "Always here," he said, a promise.

***

For a time, I hated my brother.

I kept my distance from his cradle at our house, inside my father's room, glaring at him whenever I walked nearby. When he tried to hold my hand, his hands plump and infinitesimal, I would shake them loose, tell him to back off.

For years, I couldn't forget about the evening he was born, at a hospital in Kigali miles away from our home. I was waiting outside at the end of the hall on the ground floor, the door of the room partly open. I could see my mother lying inside, on a table, beneath a sheet. There was a nurse on her right and the doctor on her left, the air a tang of antiseptics.

The nurse slipped out of the room. "You want to come in?" she asked my father, handing him a gown. He put it on and paced in. I stayed outside, twisting a rubber band with my fingers. The strand of rubber stretched and slipped from my hands, scudded across the air like a stone skimming, scratching the surface of a river.

"You killed my mother," I finally told Amata one evening, voice deepened by the glare pressed against my face, forehead creased in the darkness and gossamer mist. He laid still beside me, the tent around us flapping in the night.

He thrusted his hands out into the air, fingers clenching into fists. "It's our mother."

"Huh?" I asked, sitting up.

He picked up a rubber band from the ground, twisted it in his hands. "She's mine too."

***

We left Nyamata in the back of a lapis-blue truck of my father's friend.

The truck steered by cascades of people, pilgrims carrying white burlap sacks on rusted bicycles or on their heads, their moans lit by the rising sun.

The truck jolted down another dirt path. "Where are we going?" I asked my father.

"Do you know about the Whale?" he replied, fanning air against his face, the two of us drowning in the heat.

"The Whale?"

"There's a whale that can fly," he told me, hands splayed out in the air. "It owns a castle. That's where we are heading to now." He turned around and gazed out of the truck, at the gray sky, fallen houses with bullet-punctured walls, a man on the street behind us hobbling down the path, a cane in his hand.

"A beautiful castle," my father hummed the words into a song, "with a river, a river to swim in. And a house with a green roof, and your mother, your beautiful mother. And a castle, a castle for the four of us."

***

The day my father died at the hospital on the outskirts of the camp, I walked up to the top of the tiny hill at the center of the settlement. Amata was screaming, yelling at me to come back, but I kept on walking, a swarm of sand around my bare feet, shins scarred by weeds.

I stumbled up the path tucked between knots of blue tents, dusted and buried in dirt, past fields of withered corn that never sprouted. Halfway up the hill, rain came down, softly, then all at once.

"Look for the green roof and you'll find the way home," my father had told me once.

At the top of the hill, I looked down at the soaked land, a bare-boned child pushing a wheelbarrow down a dirt path, two shirtless men trudging across the corn fields. I thought about what he said as I tipped my head up, skin flecked by the falling rain. Silently, I listened to its rhythmic beats against the ground, the rattle syncing to my own pulse. I couldn't find any green-roofed houses.

The Neverlands

I wasn't there when they shot Luke.

I learned about it later on from one of the officers who had been there at the park with him.

They told me that he hadn't fought back. He had a Glock with him at the time, the pistol dangling by the side of his waist in his duty belt, but he didn't fire it, didn't even take it out. He just stood there, staring at the gunman and the little girl in a yellow dress beside him, when the gunman screamed and aimed at him.

They told me that the first thing he asked when he woke up in the hospital, half conscious and still dozing on and off, was whether the girl was safe now.

That evening, he died in the hospital room.

***

When Luke and I were young, we used to ride our bikes down to a bookstore in the alley behind our school. It was a minute shop, with walls painted in juniper green and a red-framed glass door, a farce of conflicting colors and nonconformity.

On summer afternoons when we were out of school, we would sit cross-legged behind its only shelf of comic books, whispering as we flipped through panels of flying superheroes combatting their villains. It was a perfect spot that we had found during a Christmas break, hidden behind the zigzags of Shakespeare and Dickens novels, where the eye could not peek from the counter.

The July we turned nine years old, we got caught by one of the customers. The man must have been in his early twenties and was draped in a leather jacket above his gray-and-white striped shirt. He had walked over without making a noise, a novel by Tolstoy in his tanned hands, and was studying the Captain America comic book we were reading. "Steve Rogers would be disappointed," he told us, lightly. We looked up from the book at him.

He eyed the old bookstore keeper who was dusting the glass door. "That Pops has a family to raise too."

We dropped the book. Our eyes traced him across the store as he paid for the novel.

The storekeeper gave him a pet on the shoulder. "Patrolling, Officer Neal?" He asked.

The young man shook his head. "It's my day off, Pops," he said, smiling, his dimples and freckles blending into one.

The storekeeper let out a laugh. "The world needs more men like you." The officer gave him a salute and walked out of the shop.

Behind our refuge of books, Luke and I sat still on the floor, the comic book we were reading on the ground between us. It was opened up to a page with Captain America giving Hitler a cuff on the face. Above him was a textbox that read JUSTICE.

***

Luke and I were born on the same day, a Wednesday in July. Upon birth, he was welcomed into a family in Tribeca, one of the most well-off neighborhoods in lower Manhattan, as an only child. My mother, on the other hand, birthed me to a family of five children, all of which were placed into foster care upon the death of my father.

Most of my childhood was spent with Luke, whose father had kindly taken me in the winter I turned three years old.

At our graduation ceremony at the police academy, a friend had come up to the two of us and studied our respective faces. Luke's hat was dotted with pieces of confetti, a bit resting on his elvish ear. She stared at me for a moment.

"I've always been wondering about this," she finally told us, her hands held up as if in surrender. "Don't take me rude, but I'm just wondering—are the two of you brothers?"

Luke and I exchanged a glance.

"I was adopted by his family," I explained to her, Luke's elbow on my shoulder. It was the first time we had told anyone the truth about my relationship with him, or rather, my non-relationship with him. "I changed my surname from Gray to White as a child."

"Oh," she said, lips parted.

"But yes," Luke told her, "Noah and I are brothers."

***

As children, Luke and I would read J.M. Barrie's *Peter Pan* aloud, lying on our stomachs on his bed as we set up our own play and acts based on the novel. For afternoons, he would be Captain Hook and I would be Peter Pan, the two of us chasing each other around in our room with paper swords. When the book had turned ragged and we had, more or less, memorized all of the lines that flowed through it, we drew our own maps of Neverland and hung them on the wall of our room.

"Never grow up," he would say, holding his knuckles out. And I would fist bump him back, our hands midair as the sun set behind us, the lights of the city caught on the window.

***

For a long time, the only coins we recognized were dimes.

It was what we carried down each sidewalk and alley, a few dimes each in the pockets of our jeans, the price for a subway token. With those coins, the entire city came under our grasp, Central Park, Bronx Zoo, Shea Stadium, and Kennedy Airport, all accessible to us.

In June and July, we spent our afternoons at the Rockaway Beach, building fortresses out of sand and planning our own treasure hunts for empty beer cans and Coca Cola bottle caps. When the weather chilled us out, we rode the bus to LaGuardia airport. There, we would stand for hours among crowds of passengers on the runways, watching planes load and take off. The first time the two of us rode the elevator to the top of the Empire State Building, we stayed there from morning till sunset.

Luke told me, looking down from the glass walls, "If there's a currency in Neverland, I bet it'll be dimes."

"Oh, the subways in Neverland won't cost you a penny," I said, being the one who was always in charge of designing and building our mythical city. "Everything's free there. Even the drinks at the malt shop."

"But Dad says with no money, you can't buy no houses," he told me.

I splayed my hands out in the air, in disbelief. "Why would they need houses? All of the folks in Neverland camp outside in the summers. They live in tents and caves under the stars. There's no need for lights or electricity."

He smiled, his freckles blending into his dimples, "That must be a good world to live in."

I stopped and stared at him for a moment, feeling a sense of familiarity within my chest.

***

My memories of my father are vague, fractured pieces that cannot be put together to form a more complete image. The truth is, all I remember about him is that his voice was resonant, deep and vibratory, like slow guitar songs that have been forgotten by people too soon and left to fade in cassette tapes.

My older brother Jack was the one who gave me most of my information about him, his stories a pool of biased realities and fabrications.

"Dad wasn't a killer," he told me on the swings one day, the two of us spending our weekly three-hours together at the park. It was the only time Jack's foster parents allowed us to meet, since he was supposed to move on instead of lingering on his past.

"He folded the best paper planes," Jack said, hopping down from the swing. "He was the fastest swimmer I know. Nobody could beat him."

But I only stared at the ground.

***

The year Luke and I turned eleven, we stopped playing Peter Pan.

A black man had raped a woman at a bar in Manhattan, just a few streets and turns from where we were living. The day after the man was imprisoned, some older kids at our school beat his son to death in the boy's bathroom. He had been one of our classmates.

"Don't you think it's actually weird?" I said one evening, lying on the floor by my bed, Barrie's book on my chest.

"Yeah?" He asked, looking down from the swiveling chair.

"Wendy was twelve or thirteen," I said. "And Peter Pan was asking her to be his mom."

He laughed at that, then rose from the chair and sat down next to me, his arms folded. "And Captain Hook too—" I went on, my hands splayed out, "why was he so obsessed with trying to murder Peter? He's just a kid, and Hook's an adult! And then there're the mermaids. They sing songs to seduce passersby and then drown their victims. Why would anyone even write that into a children's book?"

Luke shrugged and shot my arm with a rubber band. I threw the book at him. "Maybe Barrie was just trying to be realistic," he turned to gesture at the wall behind us, crayon drawings of flying whales, maps of Neverland, its castle showered in glints of violet and sapphire glitter, cone roofs and towers studded with dots of the reflected light.

"You know," he said, standing up from the floor, "in the novel, there are no nights in Neverland. No stars, ever. Because it's always daytime there."

The two of us were silent for a moment. We looked out of the window in front of us. Flashing billboards lit up the skyscrapers that enveloped the city, their blinking neon lights shadowed by the darkness above. I sat still on the rug, listening to the screeching of car tires on the streets beneath me.

***

In 1963, Eddie Lee Mays became the last subject of capital punishment in New York. Mays had been electrocuted for first-degree murder, the broadcast said, the thin air of bitter espresso hanging in the living room, Luke sitting by my side. I never told him that my father had died the same way Mays did, drowned in the hatred of our world.

For nights, after Luke fell asleep, I would sneak out of our room into the living room, sit cross-legged on the rug to read the stack of newspapers on the dining table. It was a habit, an inclination I didn't even realize I had picked up. I would spend hours reading all the articles I could on my father, attacks that called him a sadistic psychopath. Perhaps all the while, I was only trying to find that one reporter who didn't malign him, a page in the papers that would recognize him as a father of five children, a man who could fold three paper planes in a single minute.

Yet, the more I read, the more I was assured of the fact that he was maleficent, like the comic characters whom Captain America would always defeat. He was one of the villains who were half the size of the superhero, frail and frightened of their shields and suits, blows and cuffs they threw and killed people with, all in the name of justice.

***

The first time Luke and I saw the Unisphere, the circle of water foundations around the globe, we were at the World's Fair in New York at the center of a dozen exhibits, Sinclair Oil's Dinoland, the Hall of Science, and the Panorama of the city's five boroughs.

We had screamed our way down the Swiss sky ride, the two of us trying to throw each other's shoes off the cable car. We'd raced to the New York State Pavilion and exhibits where models based on society's visions for the future were showcased.

"If we have Picturephones in the future," Luke declared, scowling at the loudhailer-shaped devices that had flashing screens showing people's faces, "I'll give you all my superballs."

"If we have undersea resorts in the future, I'll give you all of my comic books," I swore.

"If we can build an international space station," he said, "I'll give you my entire Hot Wheels collection."

At the Wonder World musical, we watched a man wearing a rocket outfit fly up into the air until he was above the Unisphere. From below, he looked tiny, a dot against the sapphire sky. Unlike birds, he had no wings but two pipe-like propellers that protruded out from his suit.

The two of us gazed up at the sky. "What do you think?" I asked Luke

"I don't know," he said, after a pause. "When they told me that a man is going to fly up into the air, I was thinking about Iron Man."

I laughed. He didn't

"I thought it was going to be a superhero show," he went on, "but it's just a man who looks as scared and human as the rest of us on the ground."

I looked up at the man in the jetpack again, and the two of us stayed silent for a long time.

***

I found a photo of my father in the newspapers one evening in sixth grade.

Immediately, I cut it out and stored it in between the first and second page of *Peter Pan*. At night, I would look at it, study the features of the man in the picture, his dense eyebrows, black hair in curls down his head, the part of it that was combed nicely to the right side of his oblong-shaped face. I would stare at his smile, try to fathom its rigidness.

But what had really stuck to me was the birthmark on his brow, a port wine stain, like Gorbachev had, but much tinier, its shape like a splintered heart, the two halves a little away from each other.

Scrutinizing the picture, I had realized that I looked nothing like my father, and neither did Jack. My hair is blonde, my eyebrows thin like a strand of yarn. My face isn't angular with jagged peaks. But when I touched my forehead, I knew that I wasn't all that different, unconnected to him.

It wasn't really visible, being buried behind my bangs, but still, I couldn't ignore its existence. The birthmark I had been carrying for so long almost unconsciously, without notice or care, a port wine stain in an ovate shape, laid on my forehead. And holding the photo in my hand, I'd suddenly realized that my own birthmark looked more or less like the half of a heart.

***

For my thirteenth birthday gift, Jack gave me a pack of MDMA.

We were talking in front of my house, my hand clutching the door knob.

"Enjoy," he had said, tucking his hand into the pocket of his jeans, taking out three more packs of it. "If you want more, just tell me."

"What is this?" I asked him, sniffing the bag. I shook it next to my ear, and the things within made a crisp collision.

"Rip it open," he told me, and crossed his arms.

I tore the white package open. Inside were tablets in different colors. "Medicine?" I asked him.

"Better," he assured me, leaning close and whispering into my ear. "Ecstasy."

"It's—drugs?"

"That's right," he nodded.

I frowned. "I don't want drugs."

"Oh," he said, "don't be afraid of it. It's like candy. Only the effects are stronger. You know, the happiness."

"I don't want drugs," I told him again, handing the bag back to him.

He scoffed. "You know," he said, looking up at the door behind me, "this place has made you sissy."

"Whatever you say, Jack. I'm not going to do it." He snatched the bag back.

"Are you Peter Pan?"

"What?" I was still sniffing my hands.

"I said, are you Peter Pan?" he told me, staring me in the eyes. His overgrown hair was dotted with dandruff. "Because you never grow up!"

***

When I started high school, I asked Luke's father if I could change my last name to White, their surname. For years, I had been in a liminal space between being part of this family and being on my own. I had a mountain bike identical to Luke's and went to the same private school as him. Whatever he bought for his son, his father also gave me. But I never called anyone in the family by mother, father, or brother. I called his father Mr. White, as a student would his teacher. When I grew older, he told me to call him by his first name, Merritt.

At school, we cut Mother's Day cards out of construction paper and folded carnations out of them, adding a bit of glitter here and there. Every year, I brought them to my mother's grave with Luke. Each Father's Day, I threw my card away. I didn't want to give the paper tie to anyone.

"You know," Luke's father told me that night, "your last name, Gray—that's actually my favorite color."

"Really?"

"You see," he said, his back straightened against the couch, "it's realistic, because nothing's all white, or all black." He uncrossed his legs. "I like to think that we're living in this monochrome, Noah, where everything is shaded, some lighter and some darker. But all the while the same."

I picked at my corduroy trouser, slid my finger against the smooth lines of fabric, back and forth, again and again. The photo of my father, the one I had found in the papers so long ago, I realized, was also gray.

***

When I told Jack that I was going to be a police officer after high school, he laughed out loud. It was Christmas Eve and the two of us were sitting at a bar near midnight. The lights around us cast iridescent hums and reminded me of a kaleidoscope. He gulped down the beer in front of him, and I took another sip of my glass of water.

"The hell with that, Noah," he had told me earlier when I ordered the sparkling water. I reminded him that it was the only beverage the two of us could legally drink, but he waved the thought away with a scoff. "Why police?" he asked me after the busboy had left. The wooden chandelier lights above us shook as the door of the restaurant opened and three teenagers hurried in. The light snow outside was growing into a storm.

I tried to explain, not having the words for it, "I just thought that it would be nice—you know the feeling when you just know, so definitely and more than ever, that it's the right thing and the thing you want to do? Just that it's in your guts?"

He coughed. I didn't know whether it was from the chill in the air or at my words.

"It's for justice," I continued. "To defend it and validate its existence." My grip tightened around the coolness emanating off the glass cup in my hands. "To tell the world that it's not just some abstract ideal lying in between our minds and dreams—something that doesn't have to collide with reality, can still be true."

We left the bar, stepping into the snow, the weight of the white drapes dragging the sky down, like clothes on a clothesline. I tucked my hands into the pockets of my overcoat, and he pet my shoulder.

"You know, Noah," he said, the two of us standing still next to each other, his shadow hovering over me, "there's really no justice." His face darkened under the shadow of the night. "And I doubt there'll ever be."

***

For a long time, I was afraid of listening to the broadcast.

Before Luke and I started elementary school, the two of us would spend our mornings in the living room, playing catch-and-throw with our half-deflated soccer ball across the dining table. His father enjoyed listening to the news while eating breakfast, but I always stayed as far away as I could, dimming the words into inaudible pieces that I could not have picked up. I didn't want to hear anything about crime in New York, firearms control, homicide and shootings, or the criminals that resembled the father I once had.

"Does criminality run in blood?" I finally asked Luke one day when we were eating dinner. His parents looked up from their plates at me.

His father answered for him, "It doesn't. There's been a lot of scientific research on this, and the same conclusion has been reached repeatedly. It doesn't." He picked up the last piece of palmier on his plate, broke it in two and handed one of them to me.

I took the bit of biscuit from him, a sweet scent emanating out its sugary crust. It was the shape of a heart sliced in half.

"Your father's not a monster," he told me, rising from the seat across from me. He went to the study at the end of the hall and came back with a photo, a monochrome, like the one I had found myself. In the picture was a young woman smiling at the camera, the sunlight caught at her light-gray hair. Standing behind her, with his hands at her shoulders, was the same man I had seen in the last photo, his lips parted to a laugh.

"Your parents," Luke's father said as I studied the two figures.

I stared at the man in the photo, his black coat and tie, the peaked hat over the curls of his hair, the badge above the left side of his chest.

"Your father was charged with first-degree murder because he killed the man who raped your mother."

My lips parted, but I didn't have any words.

"Before that, your father was a policeman," he finished.

***

Luke died on a Friday in March.

The hospital he had stayed in for five hours before his death had an orange-floored hallway, wooden, the lacquer fading atop its rows of hexagons. There were foldable chairs lined up against red-framed doors.

I walked in at a little past midnight and took a seat on the chair next to the window beside his bed and stared out of it, gazing around at the city I had grown up in with him.

"You know, Luke," I told him, "you still owe me three superballs and four Hot Wheels."

He didn't say anything and I didn't expect him to. Above us, the air conditioner churned into motion.

Kaguya

The moon was pink.

Violet clouds engulfed its dim shadow and enveloped the castle around her, its karahafu scarlet and stacked above walls of mahogany stockades.

As she strolled down its hall, planks creaking under her feet, she could feel her kimono flap in the wisps of breeze. Blushing petals of the sakura trees beside her landed onto the silvery river around the castle, then coasted down the clouds into a world where they became rain.

At the end of the hallway, she stopped before a shoji, paper door, that would lead her into a room overlooking the city. The door slid open, and a silver-haired man peeked out and beckoned her in, his withered fingers trembling in the air.

"She has returned home," he proclaimed, turning back to the swarming clusters of people in front of the castle, their heads angled up at the room. "Princess," he cried, hands splayed out in the air, "Kaguya."

***

A few winds down a harbor in Nagasaki, inside a short, gray-roofed house overlooking a fish stall, Koshiro rocked the wooden cradle in front of him, kneeling on the tatami. He was humming a soft tune to himself, his black, tousled hair lit by the flickering bulb hovering above.

His son Sora ran into the bedroom, a paper plane in his hand. He burbled, mimicking the sound of airplane engines.

"Was I this tiny when I was born?" He asked Koshiro, crouching down on the tatami. Inside the cradle, his baby sister stirred. Her eyes opened, and the boy stared at them, irises darker than tar, deep and shining black like glass.

"About the same," Koshiro said, smiling. He reached his callused hand into the cradle, and his daughter thrusted hers up. Her fingers curled up around his.

The boy picked at his trousers. "Do you have to go?" he asked again. Koshiro rose from the floor, stretching his arms out.

"It's for our country," he said, his voice soft, like lyrics sung at a walking pace. The boy laid down on the tatami and listened to the whacks of the spoon against the pot in the kitchen, slices of cucumbers falling against the wooden cutting board. Soon, the door of the room slid open, and a girl walked in. She was the same age as Sora, the daughter of the fish store owner across from their house.

"Seiko!" Sora shouted and sat up from the floor. She sat down next to him, arms crossed, her white dress tucked against her.

"I'm here for another story," she smiled at him. Her short, feathery hair quivered in the air, the night breezing slipping in from the opened window. She took the paper plane from him and opened it up. He didn't argue, just watched her refold it.

"Another story?" Koshiro asked, fondling his son's hair. He pondered for a moment, scratching his chin, then sat down again on the floor. "What about a story about a princess?"

Sora laid down on the tatami, the July air skidding into his shirt. "A princess?" he contemplated.

"A princess from the moon," Koshiro said, gazing out of the window, into the darkness, past the lantern lights that studded the night sky. "A tale of a bamboo-cutter." Beside him, Seiko sharpened the folds on the paper in her hand, working her way through its jagged peaks. When she finished, she placed it onto Sora's palm. Quietly, the boy stared at the paper crane in his hand. "The story of Princess Kaguya," Koshiro said.

***

At the back of the horse-drawn carriage, rocking and skidding down the pebbled path, Kaguya sat still on her seat, gazing out the window.

"Ōjo," the coachman called her. She looked up.

He was draped in a navy-blue robe, a haori, his white trousers, its traditional folds like tides on the ebb, flapping in the air. "You don't look well," he said. She sat quietly for a moment.

"I'm alright," she said. "It's just a dream I had yesterday night."

"A dream?" The coachman asked.

She rested her head against the window, the city flashing by them. "I dreamt about the world down there. Underneath the clouds."

The carriage made a turn to the left.

"It was in ruins," she said. "There were ashes. Creeks reddened from blood." She stared at her hands. "The people said that there was a blast."

The coachman raised his lash. "It was only a dream, Kaguya-hime," he said.

But she didn't say anything. The carriage stopped in front of another castle, a shiro grander than the last one. As she was helped down the coach, she thought about her dream again. There was a boy in it, she remembered. A boy with a paper crane in his hand.

***

Inside the air raid shelter, under the tang of summer turf, Sora whistled to himself.

Seiko sat still behind him, their backs against each other's. "Kamikaze," she said suddenly.

Sora turned around. The paper crane in his hand was ragged, its beak blunt and wings sagging.

"Kamikaze pilots," she told him.

"Oh," he said. She was drawing on the dirt with a stick, figures wearing boxy aviator goggles and thick boots. "My father was one," he said.

"I know," she told him. She wrote a name down on the soiled ground, Koshiro Mashima. "Everybody did."

"I didn't," he said. Behind them, his sister walked over. She was wearing his shirt, the sleeves dangling in the air. "I thought he was only going to war for a while."

The three sat still under the summer heat, the air damp, its weight slumped down onto the ground like the petals of a wilting flower. Then suddenly, the ground started to shake. The maple trees in front of them, barely visible from their cave shelter, rocked back and forth, its limbs quaking in the air.

"What's happening?" Sora stood up from the ground but fell back down quickly. Then amidst the shuddering, something thundered out of the sky, the wave roaring across the city. Streets erupted into whiteness, light blazing their eyes. And everything went black.

***

He didn't volunteer for it.

But he wasn't forced either.

The Emperor gave speech about the country, and they were called to be the last defense. Anyone who wanted to quit this could stand up now, the sergeant said—nobody did.

"You have a son at home, right, Mashima?" one of the other pilots asked him after the assembly. There were two flags of Japan on his uniform, red circles enveloping both arms.

Koshiro took his gloves off, replying, "A daughter too. She was born a month ago."

"Oh—congrats."

"Kaguya," Koshiro said. He folded and unfolded the pair of leather gloves, its beige contour blurred in the air.

"Huh?" asked the man.

"I named her Kaguya," he told him, "after the princess in the story. The princess from the moon." He gazed up at the sky. It was gray, the color of asphalt roads, studded with a few patches of woolen clouds. "I named her Kaguya so when I'm going to fly the plane, I'll know that I'm only getting closer to her. To the moon."

***

On the hallway of a hospital in Tokyo, sky-blue floor lit by planks of LED lights above his head, a man drummed his fingers against his knees. The celadon door of the room before him was closed, and despite efforts, he could not see the doctors and nurses inside. He had the morning papers with him, folded neatly and cradled close to his ribs, locked in between his crossed arms and broad chest, but he could not read. Words came in swarming flocks before his eyes, his mind always drifting back to the hospital room, his wife inside. Silently, he counted to himself, staring at his watch.

***

She woke up.

Flecks of light studded the tatami beside her. She stretched her arms out and rose from the floor. Quietly, she opened the paper door and stepped out onto the balcony. The night above her was still dark, the silhouette of stars like strings embedded in white dye.

Underneath the lapis-blue duvet, the horizon was glittering in yellow, its contour jagged like a sharp line slicing through the clouds beneath her, beneath the castle.

"It was beautiful," she told the coachman later on in the day.

"Mm?" He asked.

She gazed out of the window of the carriage. "The sora," she said.

The sky.

***

Seiko could hear her own footsteps against the slate ground, the bouquet of chrysanthemum in her hands flapping in the air. Sora trailed behind her, his hands tucked into the pocket of his gray trousers. He was draped in a brown leather jacket.

As they turned down another path, she finally stopped before a grave. On the stone was inscribed the word *Mashima*.

Seiko took the flowers out, untying a ribbon. She handed the empty glass vase over to Sora for him to refill the water.

"You know," he said, finally taking his hands out of his pockets. She turned around. "My father named my sister Kaguya," he said, "after the princes in the folktale. She comes from the moon, he used to say a lot." She stood still. The sky above was darkening. "I think she's up there now," he went on, head back. "Up there, on the clouds. Ready to take a train over to the moon."

"Do you think she will forget us?" Seiko asked him.

"Maybe," Sora said, shrugging. "But I think she'll dream about us, from time to time.

Not to remember. Not exactly." He thought about the blast, his sister, her hair scalped off, swollen arms and bloated face. "But to never forget."

***

The door of the hospital room opened.

The man looked up from his trousers. His newspapers dropped onto the floor. A nurse walked out of it toward him, her round glasses studded with light reflected by the windows behind him.

He could see that she was smiling underneath her white mask. "Your daughter is perfectly healthy," she said. "Your wife too."

The man smiled. He knew that Seiko had always been in good health. "Your daughter," the nurse went on, "her name is—"

"Kaguya," he said, picking the papers up from the ground. "After my sister. Kaguya Mashima."

Printed in the USA
CPSIA information can be obtained
at www.ICGtesting.com
LVHW011221201223
766922LV00006B/253